The Princess and the Pea

Retold by Debbie Croft

Original by Hans Christian Andersen

Illustrations by Richard Hoit

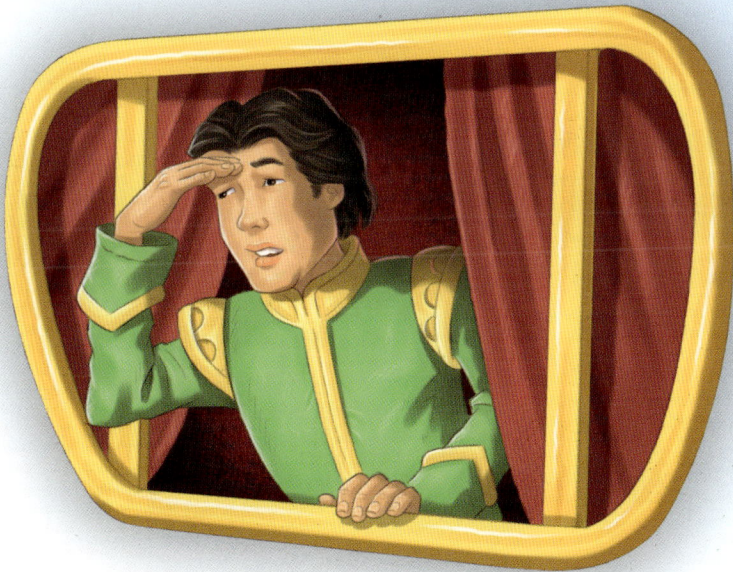

Once upon a time, there was a Prince.
He wanted to marry a beautiful princess,
but she had to be a *real* princess.

The Prince went from
one country to another,
looking for a real princess to marry.
He tried very hard.

He looked everywhere,
but he couldn't find one.

The Prince was sad.
He came home again,
but he still wanted to marry a real princess.

"There are lots of beautiful princesses,"
he said to his parents, the King and Queen.
"But I don't know if they are *real* princesses.
Every time I meet one, she tells me
that she doesn't want to leave her home
and live in our palace."

"Why not?" said the Queen, crossly.
"We have a lovely palace!"

The King smiled at the Prince and said,
"I think that a *real* princess
would want to marry a prince like you."

That night, there was a wild storm.
Lightning flashed across the sky,
and thunder rattled the windows
at the palace.
Rain was falling heavily.

Suddenly, the bell
at the palace gate rang loudly.
The King rushed out to unlock the gate.

To his surprise,
he saw a princess standing there!
She was shivering in the cold.
There was water running off her coat
and dripping down into her shoes.

"Please may I come inside?"
the princess asked the King.
"It's very cold out here,
and I'm scared of the storm."

"Yes," the King said.
"Quickly, come in out of the rain."

"I wonder if this beautiful girl
is a *real* princess?"
the King said to himself.
"Maybe the Queen will know!"

The King took the princess
into the palace
and sat her down by the fire,
where she would be warm.

He looked at the Queen,
but she didn't say anything.
She just smiled.
The Queen knew how to tell
if this girl was a real princess!

The Queen tiptoed upstairs to a bedroom. She put a tiny pea on the bottom of the bed where the princess was going to sleep that night.

Then, she lifted twenty thick mattresses and put them carefully on top of the pea. Next, she placed twenty of her best quilts on top of the mattresses.

Later that night, the princess,
who was very tired, went off to bed.
"Goodnight," the princess said
to the King and Queen,
"and thank you so much for letting me stay
in your lovely palace."

The next morning at breakfast,
the Queen asked the princess
how she had slept.

"Not very well," said the princess, sadly.
"I felt as if I was lying on something very hard,
and now my body is black and blue!"

The Queen was very happy to hear this news.
"No one but a *real* princess would feel the pea
I placed under all those mattresses!"
she said, with a smile.

All of a sudden, the rain stopped,
and the wind blew the storm clouds away.

The next day, the Prince married the Princess,
and they lived happily ever after in the palace.